The Magic of Motivation

Compiled by
Katherine Karvelas
Successories, Inc., Editorial Coordinator

CAREER PRESS
3 Tice Road, P. O. Box 687
Franklin Lakes, NJ 07417
1-800-CAREER-1; 201-848-0310 (NJ and outside U. S.)
FAX: 201-848-1727

THE MAGIC OF MOTIVATION
Cover design by Successories
Typesetting by Eileen Munson
Printed in the U.S.A. by Book-mart Press

To order this title, please call toll-free 1-800-CAREER-1 (NJ and Canada: 201-848-0310) to order using VISA or MasterCard, or for further information on books from Career Press.

Library of Congress Cataloging-in-Publication Data

The magic of motivation : quotations to empower dreams for the road to
   success / by editors of Successories.
     p.   cm.
   ISBN 1-56414-385-6 (pbk.)
    1. Motivation (Psychology)--Quotations, maxims, etc.   2. Success-
-Psychological aspects--Quotations, maxims, etc.   I. Successories.
BF503.M3 1998
153.8--dc21   98-28303

Introduction

The search for personal and professional success is a lifelong journey of trial and error. This inspiring collection of wit and wisdom is a celebration of life's lessons. Each saying is a motivational push to stay on track of your goals and pursue your dreams.

In these pages you will find more than 300 powerful and compelling quotations from a diverse group of people—business professionals, writers, activists, actors, artists, sports professionals, scientists, philosophers, politicians, and everyday people who inspire us.

This unique collection was compiled after years of insightful reading and warm discussions with people who were kind enough to share their personal collections of quotations. Working on this book has been an enlightening and gratifying experience. We hope reading these quotes will be an equally gratifying and motivating experience for you on your journey of success.

Small opportunities are often the beginning of great enterprises.

Demosthenes

I know the price of success: dedication, hard work, and an unremitting devotion to the things you want to see happen.

Frank Lloyd Wright

You cannot dream yourself into a character; you must hammer and forge yourself one.

James A. Froude

Progress always involves risk; you can't steal second base and keep your foot on first.

Fredrick Wilcox

The secret of joy in work is contained in one word—excellence. To know how to do something well is to enjoy it.

Pearl Buck

Yesterday I dared to struggle. Today I dare to win.

Bernadette Devlin

Don't wait for your ship to come
in, swim out to it.

Anonymous

The quality of a person's life is
in direct proportion to their
commitment to excellence,
regardless of their chosen field
of endeavor.

Vince Lombardi

To fly, we have to have resistance.

Maya Lin

It is no use for one to stand in
the shade and complain that the
sun does not shine upon him.
He must come out resolutely on
the hot and dusty field where
all are compelled to antagonize
with stubborn difficulties, and
pertinaciously strive until he
conquers, if he would deserve to
be crowned.

E. L. Magoon

One of the rarest things a man
ever does is to do the best he can.

Henry Wheeler Shaw

The wisest person is not the one
who has the fewest failures, but the
one who turns failures to best
account.

Richard R. Grant

If we did all the things we are
capable of doing, we would literally
astonish ourselves.

Thomas Edison

When written in Chinese, the word "crisis" is composed of two characters—one represents danger, and the other represents opportunity.

Saul David Alinsky

The price of greatness is responsibility.

Winston Churchill

Adversity reveals genius, prosperity conceals it.

Horace

Chance is always powerful. Let your hook be always cast. In the pool where you least expect it, will be a fish.

Ovid

It's kind of fun to do the impossible.

Walt Disney

Mediocre men wait for opportunity to come to them. Strong, able, alert men go after opportunity.

B. C. Forbes

If man is called to be a streetsweeper, he should sweep streets even as Michelangelo painted, or Beethoven composed music, or Shakespeare wrote poetry. He should sweep streets so well that all the hosts of heaven and earth will pause to say, here lived a great streetsweeper who did his job well.

Martin Luther King, Jr.

Nature gave men two ends—one
to sit on and one to think with.
Ever since then man's success or
failure has been dependent on the
one he used most.

George R. Kirkpatrick

Do not follow where the path may
lead. Go instead where there is
no path and leave a trail. Only
those who will risk going too far
can possibly find out how far one
can go.

T. S. Eliot

Man's mind, once stretched by a
new idea, never regains its original
dimensions.

Oliver Wendell Holmes

The future belongs to those who
believe in the beauty of their
dreams.

Eleanor Roosevelt

The reward of a thing well done is
to have done it.

Ralph Waldo Emerson

Put your heart, mind, intellect, and soul even to your smallest acts. This is the secret of success.

Swami Sivananda

The glory of success is not in never falling, but in *rising* every time we fall.

Anonymous

The journey of a thousand leagues begins from beneath your feet.

Lao-tse

H*ow do you go from where you are to where you want to be? I think you have to have an enthusiasm for life. You have to have a dream, a goal, and you have to be willing to work for it.*

Jim Valvano

I am not the smartest or most talented person in the world, but I succeeded because I keep going, and going, and going.

Sylvester Stallone

To do an evil action is base; to do a good action, without incurring danger, is common enough. But it is part of a good man to do great and noble deeds though he risks everything.

Plutarch

No one succeeds without effort.
Those who succeed owe their
success to their perseverance.

Ramana Maharishi

Reach where you cannot.

Anonymous

The difficulties and struggles of
today are but the price we must
pay for the accomplishments and
victories of tomorrow.

William J. H. Boetcker

Little minds are tamed and subdued by misfortune; but great minds rise above them.

Washington Irving

An idea is salvation by imagination.

Frank Lloyd Wright

Perseverance is a great element of success. If you only knock long enough and loud enough at the gate, you are sure to wake up somebody.

Henry Wadsworth Longfellow

What is the recipe for successful achievement? To my mind there are just four essential ingredients: Choose a career you love. Give it the best there is in you. Seize your opportunities. And be a member of the team.

Benjamin F. Fairless

The Wright brothers flew right
through the smoke of impossibility.

Charles F. Kettering

Great hopes make great men.

Thomas Fuller

Genius is one percent inspiration,
and ninety-nine percent
perspiration.

Thomas Edison

Success comes before work only in the dictionary.

Anonymous

Making the simple complicated is commonplace; making the complicated simple, awesomely simple, that's creativity.

Charles Mingus

The sure way to miss success is to miss the opportunity.

Victor Chasles

Do it big or stay in bed.

Larry Kelly

There is one thing stronger than
all the world, and that is an idea
whose time has come.

Victor Hugo

The only way to discover the limits
of the possible is to go beyond
them into the impossible.

Arthur C. Clarke

There is no upper limit to what individuals are capable of doing with their minds. There is no age limit that bars them from beginning. There is no obstacle that cannot be overcome if they persist and believe.

H. G. Wells

Continuous efforts—not strength or intelligence—is the key to unlocking our potential.

Winston Churchill

Future favors the bold.

Virgil

Accept the challenges, so that you may feel the exhilaration of victory.

George S. Patton

Find a need and fill it.

Anonymous

Nothing worthwhile comes easily.
Half effort does not produce half
results. It produces no results.
Work, continuous work and hard
work, is the only way to accomplish
results that last.

Hamilton Holt

The secret of success is constancy
of purpose.

Benjamin Disraeli

Thoughts lead on to purposes;
purposes go forth in action;
actions form habits; habits decide
character; and character fixes our
destiny.

Tyron Edwards

Luck is what happens when
preparation meets opportunity.

Elmer Letterman

No problem can stand the assault
of sustained thinking.

Voltaire

Be of a good cheer. Do not think of today's failures, but of the success that may come tomorrow. You have set yourselves a difficult task, but you will succeed if you persevere; and you will find a joy in overcoming obstacles. Remember, no effort that we make to attain something beautiful is ever lost.

Helen Keller

If you want to succeed, you must make your own opportunities as you go.

John B. Gough

I was not a winner when I first came out on tour. I had to develop a trust in myself that I had the ability to win.

Thomas J. Watson

When two men in a business always agree, one of them is unnecessary.

Anonymous

No great thing is created suddenly.

Epictetus

Before everything else, getting
success is more a function of
consistent common sense than it
is of genius.

An Wang

I can't imagine a person becoming
a success who doesn't give this
game of life everything he's got.

Walter Cronkite

Every man is the architect of his own fortune.

Appius Claudius

If you *dream* it, you can *do* it.

Walt Disney

Every worthwhile accomplishment, big or little, has its stages of drudgery and triumph; a beginning, a struggle, and a victory.

Anonymous

I *do the best I know how, the very best I can; and I mean to keep on doing it to the end. If the end brings me out all right, what is said against me will not amount to anything. If the end brings me out all wrong, ten angels swearing I was right would make no difference.*

Abraham Lincoln

Before everything else, getting
ready is the secret of success.

Henry Ford

Nothing splendid had ever been
achieved except by those who
dared believe that something
inside them was superior to
circumstance.

Bruce Barton

It may be that those who do the
most, dream the most.

Anonymous

Lack of money is no obstacle. Lack of an idea is an obstacle.

Ken Hakuta

Act quickly and think slowly.

Greek proverb

Success is not so much achievement as achieving. Refuse to join the cautious crowd that plays not to lose; play to win.

David J. Mahoney

We write our own destiny. We
become what we do.

Madame Chiang Kai-Shek

There is something that is much
more scarce, something rarer than
ability. It is the ability to recognize
ability.

Robert Half

It is not enough to aim; you must
hit.

Italian proverb

Few will have the greatness
to bend history itself, but each
of us can work to change a
small portion of events, and in
the total of all those acts will be
written the history of this
generation.

Robert F. Kennedy

If one advances confidently in the direction of his dreams, and endeavors to live the life which he has imagined, he will meet with success unexpected in common hours.

Henry David Thoreau

Nothing great will ever be achieved without great men, and men are great only if they are determined to be so.

Charles de Gaulle

Don't bunt. Aim out of the ball park. Aim for the company of the immortals.

David Ogilvy

Why not go out on a limb? Isn't that where the fruit is?

Frank Scully

It is the old lesson—worthy purpose, patient energy for its accomplishment, a resoluteness undaunted by difficulties.

W. Punshon

It is the constant and determined effort that breaks down all resistance, sweeps away all obstacles.

Claude M. Bristol

Never give up and never give in.

Hubert H. Humphrey

To know what to do is wisdom. To know how to do it is skill. But doing it, as it should be done, tops the other two virtues.

Anonymous

The world judges you by what you have done, not by what you have started out to do; by what you have completed, not by what you have begun. The bulldog wins by simple expedient of holding on to the finish.

Baltasar Gracián

A person who walks in another's
tracks leaves no footprints.

Anonymous

In the performance of a good
action, a man not only benefits
himself, but he confers a blessing
upon others.

Sir Philip Sidney

Let me win, but if I cannot win, let
me be brave in the attempt.

Special Olympics motto

Don't learn the tricks of the trade.
Learn the trade.

Anonymous

When your work speaks for itself,
don't interrupt.

Henry J. Kaiser

Make up your mind to act
decidedly and take the
consequences. No good is ever
done in this world by hesitation.

Thomas Henry Huxley

Chance favors the prepared mind.

Louis Pasteur

When you are trying to get something done, don't worry too much about stepping on someone else's toes. Nobody gets his toes stepped on unless he is standing still or sitting down on the job.

Anonymous

Many receive advice, only the wise profit from it.

Syrus

Nothing in the world can take
the place of persistence. Talent will
not; nothing is more common than
unsuccessful men with talent.
Genius will not; unrewarded
genius is almost a proverb.
Education will not; the world
is full of educated derelicts.
Persistence and determination
alone are omnipotent.

Calvin Coolidge

There is no such thing in anyone's
life as an unimportant day.

Alexander Woollcott

He who refuses to embrace a
unique opportunity loses the prize
as surely as if he had failed.

William James

A successful person is a dreamer
who someone believed in.

Anonymous

The only good luck many great men ever had was being born with the ability and determination to overcome bad luck.

Channing Pollock

We will not know unless we begin.

Howard Zinn

A single conversation across the table with a wise man is worth a month's study of books.

Chinese proverb

Far away there in the sunshine are my highest aspirations. I may not reach them, but I can look up and see their beauty, believe in them and try to follow where they may lead.

Louisa May Alcott

Obstacles are those frightful things you see when you take your eyes off your goals.

Anonymous

> At the root of human responsibility is the concept of perfection, the urge to achieve it, the intelligence to find a path towards it, and the will to follow the path, if not to the end at least the distance needed to rise above individual limitations and environmental impediments.
>
> **Aung San Su Kyi**

You will become as small as your controlling desire; as great as your dominant aspiration.

James Allen

When you hire people who are smarter than you are, you prove you are smarter than they are.

R. H. Grant

Genius is the ability to reduce the complicated to the simple.

C. W. Ceran

Things may come to those who
wait, but only the things left by
those who hustle.

Abraham Lincoln

Winners expect to win in advance.
Life is a self-fulfilling prophecy.

Anonymous

Your big opportunity may be right
where you are now.

Napoleon Hill

Try out your ideas by visualizing
them in action.

David Seabury

Things turn out the best for the
people who make the best of the
way things turn out.

John Wooden

The whole world steps aside for
the man who knows where he is
going.

Anonymous

Winning is not a sometime thing; it's an all time thing. You don't win once in a while, you don't do things right once in a while, you do them right all the time. Winning is a habit. Unfortunately, so is losing.

Vince Lombardi

It often requires more courage to dare to do right than to fear to do wrong.

Abraham Lincoln

Success is a journey, not a destination.

Anonymous

Failure is the opportunity to begin again more intelligently.

Henry Ford

He who believes is strong; he who doubts is weak. Strong convictions precede great actions.

J. F. Clarke

The mind is like a parachute—it doesn't work unless it's open.

Anonymous

The secret of happiness is not doing what one likes, but in liking what one does.

James M. Barrie

I've always believed that anybody with a little ability, a little guts and the desire to apply himself can make it.

Willie Shoemaker

Well done is better than well said.

Ben Franklin

Our chief want in life is somebody who will make us do what we can.

Ralph Waldo Emerson

One hour of life, crowded to the full with glorious action, and filled with noble risks, is worth whole years of those mean observances of paltry decorum, in which men steal through existence, like the sluggish waters through a marsh, without either honour or observation.

Sir Walter Scott

A great pleasure in life is doing
what people say you cannot do.

Walter Gagehot

The man who believes he can do
something is probably right, and
so is the man who believes he can't.

Anonymous

One man with courage makes a
majority.

Andrew Jackson

The difference between a
successful person and others is
not a lack of strength, not a lack
of knowledge, but rather in a lack
of will.

Vince Lombardi

Enthusiasm without knowledge is
like haste in the dark.

Anonymous

Yesterday is a cancelled check;
tomorrow is a promissory note;
today is the only cash you
have—so spend it wisely.

Kay Lyons

The kind of people I look for to fill top management spots are the eager beavers, the mavericks. These are the guys who try to do more than they are expected to do—they always reach.

Lee Iacocca

The only way to enjoy anything in this life is to earn it first.

Ginger Rogers

This became a credo of mine...attempt the impossible in order to improve your work.

Bette Davis

The most important thing about a man is what he believes in the depth of his being. This is the thing that makes him what he is, the thing that organizes him and feeds him; the thing that keeps him going in the face of untoward circumstances; the thing that gives him resistance and drive.

Hugh Stevenson Tigner

Failures are divided into two classes—those who thought and never did, and those who did and never thought.

John Salak

The man who wins may have been counted out several times, but he didn't hear the referee.

H. E. Jansen

In great attempts it is glorious even to fail.

Anonymous

The path to success is to take
massive, determined action.

Anthony Robbins

The ultimate measure of a man is
not where he stands in moments of
comfort and convenience, but
where he stands at times of
challenge and controversy.

Martin Luther King, Jr.

In every failure is the seed of
success.

Anonymous

The people who get on in this world are the people who get up and look for the circumstances they want, and, if they can't find them, make them.

George Bernard Shaw

The work praises the man.

Irish proverb

The will to succeed is important, but what's even more important is the will to prepare.

Bobby Knight

Nothing is impossible; there are ways that lead to everything, and if we had sufficient will we should always have sufficient means. It is often merely for an excuse that we say things are impossible.

Francois de la Rochefoucauld

Pick battles big enough to matter,
small enough to win.

Jonathan Kozel

The human spirit will overcome
any obstacles in the way of a
dream.

Anonymous

The nerve that never relaxes, the
eye that never blenches, the
thought that never wanders, these
are the masters of victory.

Edmund Burke

A hunch is creativity trying to tell
you something.

Anonymous

If you wish to succeed in life, make
perseverance your bosom friend,
experience your wise counselor,
caution your elder brother, and
hope your guardian genius.

Joseph Addison

Opportunities multiply as they are
seized.

Sun Tzu

Live daringly, boldly, fearlessly.
Taste the relish to be found in
competition—in having put forth
the best within you.

Henry Kaiser

To keep a lamp burning we have to
keep putting oil in it.

Mother Teresa

There are no secrets to success. It
is the result of preparation, hard
work, and learning from failure.

Colin L. Powell

B*ear in mind, if you are going to amount to anything, that your success does not depend upon the brilliancy and the impetuosity with which you take hold, but upon the everlasting and sanctified bulldoggedness with which you hang on after you have taken hold.*

Dr. A. B. Meldrum

It is a funny thing about life: If you refuse to accept anything but the very best, you very often get it.

Somerset Maugham

He who never fell never climbed.

Anonymous

It is difficult to say what is impossible, for the dream of yesterday is the hope of today and the reality of tomorrow.

Robert H. Goddard

The worst bankrupt in the world
is the person who has lost his
enthusiasm.

H. W. Arnold

Do not wish to be anything but
what you are, and try to be that
perfectly.

St. Francis De Sales

To love what you do and feel that it
matters—how could anything be
more fun?

Katharine Graham

All mankind is divided into three classes: those that are immovable, those that are movable, and those that move.

Arabian proverb

Just go out there and do what you've got to do.

Martina Navratilova

The highest reward for a person's toil is not what they get for it, but what they become by it.

John Ruskin

D*id is a word of achievement,*

Won't is a word of retreat,

Might is a word of bereavement,

Can't is a word of defeat,

Ought is a word of duty,

Try is a word each hour,

Will is a word of beauty,

Can is a word of power.

Anonymous

Life affords no higher pleasure
than that of surmounting
difficulties, passing from one step
of success to another, forming new
wishes and seeing them gratified.

Samuel Jackson

No one ever stumbled onto
something big while sitting down.

Anonymous

Dollars have never been known to
produce character, and character
will never be produced by money.

W. K. Kellogg

We must use time creatively—and
forever realize that the time is
always hope to do great things.

Martin Luther King, Jr.

You hit home runs not by chance,
but by preparation.

Roger Maris

There are two ways of exerting
one's strength: One is pushing
down, the other is pulling up.

Booker T. Washington

Unless you choose to do great things with it, it makes no difference how much you are rewarded, or how much power you have.

Oprah Winfrey

The past is behind us and the future lies ahead.

Irwin Corey

You never really lose until you quit trying.

Mike Ditka

Some men give up their designs when they have almost reached the goal; while others, on the contrary, obtain a victory by exerting at the last moment more vigorous efforts than before.

Polybius

He who is not courageous enough
to take risks will accomplish
nothing in life.

Muhammad Ali

Those who act receive the prizes.

Aristotle

Push yourself again and again.
Don't give an inch until the final
buzzer sounds.

Larry Bird

He who makes great demands on
himself is naturally inclined to
make great demands on others.

André Gide

There are really no mistakes in
life—only lessons.

Anonymous

Great spirits have always
encountered violent opposition
from mediocre minds.

Albert Einstein

People forget how fast you did a job—but they remember how well you did it.

Howard W. Newton

When everybody said I'd never be any good again, it just made me push on.

Evonne Goolagong

Success seems to be largely a matter of hanging on after others have let go.

William Feather

All that is necessary to break the spell of inertia and frustration is this: Act as if it were impossible to fail. That is the talisman, the formula, the command of right-about-face which turns us from failure towards success.

Dorothea Brande

Life shrinks or expands in
proportion to one's courage.

Anaïs Nin

Take a chance! All life is a chance.
The man who goes farthest is
generally the one who is willing to
do and dare.

Dale Carnegie

We conquer—not in any brilliant
fashion—we conquer by
continuing.

George Matheson

No bird soars too high, if he soars
with his own wings.

Ralph Waldo Emerson

Every action of our lives touches on
some chord that will vibrate in
eternity.

Edwin Hubbel Chapin

I was successful because you
believed in me.

Ulysses S. Grant, to Abraham Lincoln

Victory won't come to me unless I go to it.

Marianne Moore

I learned that the only way you are going to get anywhere in life is to work hard at it. If you do, you'll win—if you don't, you won't.

Bruce Jenner

To win you have to risk loss.

Jean-Claude Killy

There is genius in persistence.
It conquers all opposers. It gives
confidence. It annihilates
obstacles. Everybody believes in
a determined man. People know
that when he undertakes a thing,
the battle is half won, for his rule
is to accomplish whatever he sets
out to do.

Orison Swett Marden

It is necessary to try to surpass oneself always; this occupation ought to last as long as life.

Christina, Queen of Sweden

One important key to success is self-confidence. An important key to self-confidence is preparation.

Arthur Ashe

Becoming number one is easier than remaining number one.

Bill Bradley

People often ask me if I know the secret of success and if I could tell others how to make their dreams come true. My answer is…you do it by working.

Walt Disney

The secret of success for every person who has been successful lies in the fact that he formed the habit of doing those things that failures don't like to do.

A. Jackson King

High expectations are the key to everything.

Sam Walton

The first requisite for success is the ability to apply your physical and mental energies to one problem incessantly without growing weary.

Thomas Edison

The actions of men are the best interpreters of their thoughts.

John Locke

F*our short words sum up*
what has lifted most successful
individuals above the crowd:
a little bit more. They did all
that was expected of them
and a little bit more.

A. Lou Vickery

Those who dare to fail miserably,
can achieve greatly.

Robert F. Kennedy

The greatest pleasure in life
is doing what people say you
cannot do.

Anonymous

Difficulties mastered are
opportunities won.

Winston Churchill

Dreams are the touchstones of our character.

Henry David Thoreau

The fact is that life is either hard and satisfying or easy and unsatisfying.

Richard Leider

It is the docile who achieve the most impossible things in this world.

Rabindranath Tagore

The merit of an action lies in
finishing it to the end.

Genghis Khan

Nothing in life is more exciting
and rewarding than the sudden
flash of insight that leaves you a
changed person—not only
changed, but for the better.

Arthur Gordon

Every really new idea looks crazy
at first.

Alfred North Whitehead

Motivation is everything.
You can do the work of two
people, but you can't be two
people. Instead, you have to
inspire the next guy down the
line and get him to inspire his
people.

Lee Iacocca

Don't wait for extraordinary opportunities. Seize common occasions and make them great.

Orison Swett Marden

Don't let the fear of striking out hold you back.

Babe Ruth

No man ever became great except through many and great mistakes.

William Ewart Gladstone

Do just once what others say you can't do, and you will never pay attention to their limitations again.

James R. Cook

It is not enough to do your best; you must know what to do, and *then* do your best.

W. Edwards Deming

No one ever gets far unless he accomplishes the impossible at least once a day.

Elbert Hubbard

The impossible is often the untried.

Jim Goodwin

What looks like a loss may be the very event which is subsequently responsible for helping to produce the major achievement of your life.

Srully Blotnick

Success is the maximum utilization of the ability that you have.

Zig Ziglar

When you are inspired by some great purpose, some extraordinary project, all your thoughts break their bounds: Your mind transcends limitations, your consciousness expands in every direction, and you find yourself in a new, great, and wonderful world. Dormant forces, faculties, and talents become alive, and you discover yourself to be a greater person by far than you ever dreamed yourself to be.

Patanjali

If you want to conquer fear, don't sit home and think about it. Go out and get busy.

Dale Carnegie

Even a mistake may turn out to be the one thing necessary to a worthwhile achievement.

Henry Ford

We are continually faced by great opportunities brilliantly disguised as insoluble problems.

Anonymous

When your desires are strong
enough you will appear to possess
superhuman powers to achieve.

Napolean Hill

Whatever is worth doing at all is
worth doing well.

Earl of Chesterfield

An invincible determination can
accomplish almost anything and
in this lies the great distinction
between great men and little men.

Thomas Fuller

Nothing good comes in life or athletics unless a lot of hard work has preceded the effort. Only temporary success is achieved by taking shortcuts.

Roger Staubach

Character is a victory, not a gift.

Anonymous

I never knew a man come to greatness or eminence who lay abed late in the morning.

Jonathan Swift

We get mostly what we go after—if we go after it hard enough. About the only thing that has ever come into our life without effort is trouble; and much of that can be traced to a desire to take hold of the blossoms instead of the branches.

Anonymous

The heights by great men reached were not attained by sudden flight, but they, while their companions slept, were toiling upward in the night.

Henry Wadsworth Longfellow

One man has enthusiasm for 30 minutes, another for 30 days, but it is the man who has it for 30 years who makes a success of his life.

Edward B. Butler

Resolve that whatever you do, you will bring the whole man to it; that you will fling the whole weight of your being into it.

Orison Swett Marden

The path to success is to take massive, determined action.

Anthony Robbins

If you want something done, ask a busy person to do it. The more things you do, the more you can do.

Lucille Ball

The man who is waiting for
something to turn up might start
on his shirt sleeves.

Garth Henrichs

Make stepping stones out of
stumbling blocks.

Jack Penn

The greatest achievement of the
human spirit is to live up to one's
opportunities and make the most
of one's resources.

Vauvenargues

A *price has to be paid for success. Almost invariably those who have reached the summits worked harder and longer, studied and planned more assiduously, practiced more self-denial, overcame more difficulties than those of us who have not risen so far.*

B. C. Forbes

You cannot achieve a new goal by applying the same level of thinking that got you where you are today.

Albert Einstein

The difference between ordinary and extraordinary is that little extra.

Anonymous

Nothing great was ever achieved without enthusiasm.

Ralph Waldo Emerson

No great thing is created suddenly.

Epictetus

If you aren't fired with enthusiasm,
you will be fired with enthusiasm.

Vince Lombardi

When asked how he conquered the
world, Alexander the Great
replied: "By not delaying."

Anonymous

Persistent people begin their
success where others end in
failures.

Edward Eggleston

Great works are performed not by
strength, but perseverance.

Samuel Johnson

If you got the guts to stick it out,
you are going to make it.

Brian Hays

As in the case in all branches
of art, success depends in a very
large measure upon individual
initiative and exertion, and
cannot be achieved except by
dint of hard work.

Anna Pavlova

How many a man has thrown up his hands at a time when a little more effort, a little more patience would have achieved success?

Elbert Hubbard

Destiny is not a matter of chance, it is a matter of choice.

Anonymous

You become a champion by fighting one more round. When things are tough, you fight one more round.

James Corbett

Valor grows by daring, fear by holding back.

Syrus

To be what we are, and to become what we are capable of becoming, is the only end of life.

Robert Louis Stevenson

Only learn to seize good fortune, for good fortune is always here.

Goethe

When a man is willing and eager,
the gods join in.

Aeschylus

The trick is not how well you deal
with success, but how well you deal
with adversity.

W. Michael Blumenthal

Knowledge is power, but
enthusiasm pulls the switch.

Ivern Ball

Often the difference between a successful person and a failure is not one's better abilities or ideas, but the courage that one has to bet on one's ideas, to take a calculated risk—and to act.

Maxwell Maltz

Boldness has genius, power, and magic in it. Begin it now.

Goethe

Nothing can resist the human will that will stake even its existence on its stated purpose.

Benjamin Disraeli

Success is simply a matter of luck. Ask any failure.

Anonymous

Success consists of going from
failure to failure without loss of
enthusiasm.

William S. Churchill

You may have to fight a battle
more than once to win it.

Margaret Thatcher

The majority of men meet with
failure because of their lack of
persistence in creating new plans
to take the place of those which
fail.

Napoleon Hill

Choices are the hinges of destiny.

Anonymous

There is no road to success but through a clear strong purpose. Nothing can take its place. A purpose underlies character, culture, position, attainment of every part.

T. T. Munger

Success doesn't come to you...you go to it.

Marva Collins

The road to happiness lies in two simple principles: Find what it is that interests you and that you can do well, and when you find it put your soul into it—every bit of energy and ambition and natural ability you have.

John D. Rockefeller

We shall win because we are the stronger.

Paul Reynaud

The difference between what we do and what we are capable of doing would solve most of the world's problems.

Gandhi

Just as iron rusts from disuse, even so does inaction spoil the intellect.

Leonardo da Vinci

Do not live in the fear of what the future may hold. Live in the anticipation of the new opportunities that lie ahead.

Anonymous

Strength does not come from physical capacity. It comes from indomitable will.

Jawharlal Nehru

I go where the puck is going to be, not where the puck is.

Wayne Gretzky

It is easy to sit up and take notice.
What is difficult is getting up and
taking action.

Al Batt

Success doesn't mean the absence
of failures; it means the attainment
of ultimate objectives. It means
winning the war, not every battle.

Edward Bliss

Never despair, keep pushing on!

Sir Thomas Lipton

When I was a child, my mother said to me, "If you become a soldier you'll be a general. If you become a monk you'll end up as the Pope." Instead I became a painter and wound up as Picasso.

Pablo Picasso

Every person who wins in any undertaking must be willing to cut all sources of retreat. Only by doing so can one be sure of maintaining the state of mind known as a burning desire to win.

Napoleon Hill

Successful people have learned to make themselves do the thing that has to be done when it has to be done, whether they like it or not.

Aldous Huxley

The real secret of success is
enthusiasm.

Walter Chrysler

Many of life's failures are people
who did not realize how close they
were to success when they gave up.

Thomas Edison

If you get up one more time than
you fall you will make it through.

Chinese proverb

You don't have to stay up nights to succeed; you have to stay awake days.

Earl Nightingale

The greater the difficulty, the greater the glory.

Cicero

The only joy in the world is to begin.

Cesare Pavese

Do more than exist, live.

Do more than touch, feel.

Do more than look, observe.

Do more than read, absorb.

Do more than hear, listen.

Do more than think, ponder.

Do more than talk, say something.

John H. Rhoades

Nothing is impossible to the man
who can will, and then do; this is
the only law of success.

Mirabeau

Happiness lies in the joy of
achievement and the thrill of
creative effort.

Franklin Roosevelt

A problem is a chance for you to
do your best.

Duke Ellington

The mind is not a vessel to be
filled, but a fire to be kindled.

Plutarch

Abilities not used are abilities
wasted.

Anonymous

It is one of the most beautiful
compensations of this life that no
man can sincerely try to help
another without helping himself.

Ralph Waldo Emerson

These other Successories® titles are available from Career Press:

➤ *The Essence of Attitude*

➤ *The Power of Goals*

➤ *Commitment to Excellence*

➤ *Winning with Teamwork*

➤ *The Best of Success*

To order call: 1-800-CAREER-1

These other Successories® titles are available from Career Press:

- ➤ *Great Little Book on The Gift of Self-Confidence*
- ➤ *Great Little Book on The Peak Performance Woman*
- ➤ *Great Little Book on Mastering Your Time*
- ➤ *Great Little Book on Effective Leadership*
- ➤ *Great Little Book on Personal Achievement*
- ➤ *Great Little Book on Successful Selling*
- ➤ *Great Little Book on Universal Laws of Success*

- ➤ *Great Quotes from Great Women*
- ➤ *Great Quotes from Great Sports Heroes*
- ➤ *Great Quotes from Great Leaders*
- ➤ *Great Quotes from Zig Ziglar*

To order call: 1-800-CAREER-1